DATE DUE

EDGE BOOKS™

TRUE TALES OF
SURVIVAL
PRESENTS:

DISASTER IN THE MOUNTAINS!

COLBY COOMBS'
STORY OF SURVIVAL

by Tim O'Shei

Consultant:
Al Siebert, PhD
Author of *The Survivor Personality*

★

Capstone
press

Mankato, Minnesota

Edge Books are published by Capstone Press,
151 Good Counsel Drive, P.O. Box 669, Mankato, Minnesota 56002.
www.capstonepress.com

Library of Congress Cataloging-in-Publication Data
O'Shei, Tim.
    Disaster in the mountains!: Colby Coombs' story of survival / by Tim O'Shei.
    p. cm.—(Edge books. True tales of survival)
    Summary: "Describes how mountain climber Colby Coombs survived an
avalanche in the Alaskan mountains"—Provided by publisher.
    Includes bibliographical references and index.
    ISBN-13: 978-0-7368-6778-8 (hardcover)
    ISBN-10: 0-7368-6778-3 (hardcover)
    ISBN-13: 978-0-7368-7868-5 (softcover pbk.)
    ISBN-10: 0-7368-7868-8 (softcover pbk.)
    1. Mountaineering accidents—Alaska—Foraker, Mount—Juvenile literature.
2. Wilderness survival—Alaska—Foraker, Mount—Juvenile literature.
3. Avalanches—Alaska—Foraker, Mount—Juvenile literature. 4. Coombs,
Colby—Juvenile literature. I. Title. II. Series.
GV199.42.A42F666 2007
796.52'2—dc22   2006024767

Editorial Credits
Angie Kaelberer, editor; Jason Knudson, designer; Wanda Winch,
    photo researcher/photo editor

Photo Credits
AccentAlaska.com/Dwayne King, 26–27
©Alaska Mountaineering School Collection, 14–15, 20, 28
©Colby Coombs Collection, 10 (both), 13, 16
Comstock, 2–3, 12–13 (background)
Corbis/Galen Rowell, 6–7, 8: Kevin T. Gilbert, 22–23; Paul A. Souders, 18–19;
    Royalty-Free, front cover, 4–5 (background), 10–11 (background), 20–21
    (background), 24–25 (background),
Rex Rystedt Photography, SeattlePhoto.com, 4
Sayre Coombs, 29
Shutterstock/Jan Bruder, back cover; Marco Regalia, 30–31; Michele Perbellini, 1, 32;
    Remi Cauzid, 28–29 (background)
WorldFoto/Paul A. Souders, 25

1 2 3 4 5 6 12 11 10 09 08 07

TABLE OF CONTENTS

CHAPTER 1

A DANGEROUS CLIMB

LEARN ABOUT:

- THREE FRIENDS
- DISASTER
- DEAD OR ALIVE?

4

At age 25, Colby Coombs was a skilled mountain climber.

Step, step, ax. Step, step, ax.

Colby Coombs climbed the mountain slowly and carefully, following that three-step pattern. Step with one foot. Step with the other foot. Balance yourself with the ax. Step, step, ax. One. Two. Three.

Colby was climbing Mount Foraker. The 17,400-foot (5,300-meter) mountain is part of Denali National Park in Alaska. Colby's friend Ritt Kellogg was 150 feet (46 meters) below him. Another friend, Tom Walter, was 150 feet above him. The climbers were at an elevation of about 13,200 feet (4,000 meters).

The snow was so thick that Colby couldn't see either of his friends. But he could feel them moving, because the three men were tied together by ropes. The rope connecting Colby to Tom was taut. That was good, because a tight rope meant Tom was moving safely upward.

Suddenly, Tom's rope loosened. Colby instantly knew something was wrong. Within seconds, a huge mass of snow and ice shoved Colby off his feet. He fell faster than he could ever have imagined. Seconds later, he blacked out.

When he woke up hours later, Colby was confused, cold, and frightened. He slowly realized what had happened. An avalanche had knocked the climbers down the mountain. Colby was injured, but alive. He wasn't sure about his friends.

Within moments, a huge mass of snow and ice knocked Colby off his feet. He fell faster than he could ever have imagined.

An avalanche like this one slammed into Colby and his friends.

CHAPTER 2

A FATEFUL DAY

LEARN ABOUT:
- A GREAT START
- FIGHTING BLIZZARDS
- TURNING BACK

Colby, Ritt, and Tom began their climb at Kahiltna Glacier base camp.

The months of May, June, and July are ideal for climbing the Alaska Range. With sunlight nearly all day and night, the air stays warm enough for people to survive. But temperatures are cold enough to keep snow and ice from constantly melting, which can cause avalanches.

Colby, Ritt, and Tom began their trip at a base camp near the Kahiltna Glacier landing strip in Denali National Park. They set up tents and a small kitchen. They made spaghetti for dinner and buried the leftovers in the snow to enjoy when they returned. For breakfast, they feasted on pancakes. The men ate a lot at base camp, knowing they would eat very little during the climb.

SETTING OFF

On June 14, 1992, the friends left the camp and traveled 4 miles (6.4 kilometers) across the glacier to Mount Foraker. As the friends reached the mountain base, a blizzard hit. They decided to spend the night there and wait out the storm.

9

Tom Walter was the most experienced climber of the group.

Ritt Kellogg had been Colby's best friend since college.

EDGE FACT

The path Colby and his friends took up the mountain was called the Pink Panther. The first group to climb it carried a stuffed toy panther for luck.

Colby and Ritt slept huddled in a small tent. Tom dug a small cave in the snow. He slept in an outdoor sleeping bag called a bivvy bag.

Around noon the next day, the friends were ready to begin their climb. They left a red plastic sled and their skis at the bottom of the mountain. The climbers were loaded with ropes, ice axes, a tent, a small stove, and enough food and stove fuel for six days.

Climbing the steep cliffs and frozen rocks was challenging. Spiky metal frames called crampons on their boots helped the men navigate the mountainside. They also used ice axes and even their bare hands.

Despite the conditions, the climbers reached an elevation of 10,000 feet (3,000 meters) that day. Other climbers had taken three days to reach this point. The friends celebrated by setting up camp, sipping hot soup, and getting some sleep.

STORMY SIGNS

Colby, Ritt, and Tom made good progress on June 16. But that night, another snowstorm hit. The men decided to set up camp. They stayed put until midday on June 18, when the weather began to clear.

The next portion of the climb was especially steep. As the threesome struggled up the rocks, the weather turned bad again. The snow made it too difficult for the climbers to reach the summit. They decided to move a little higher to the mountain's southeast ridge. They could safely camp there that night and then head back to base camp. They connected 165-foot (50-meter) ropes to each other. Tom was first, then Colby, then Ritt.

It was early in the morning of June 19—the day that would change Colby Coombs' life.

In the snow cave, Tom heated soup for supper.

13

CHAPTER 3

THE LONG WAY DOWN

LEARN ABOUT:

- A HEARTBREAKING DISCOVERY
- THE WILL TO SURVIVE
- A PAINFUL DESCENT

14

Mount Foraker is the sixth-tallest peak in North America.

The last thing Colby remembered was Tom's rope going slack. As Colby tumbled down the mountain, he lost consciousness. When he awoke hours later, he hung limply from his rope. Colby saw Tom hanging less than 10 feet (3 meters) away. A streak of blood dripped far down the cliff. Colby knew that wasn't good.

Colby didn't realize it, but he had fallen 1,000 feet (300 meters). His body was screaming with pain. Colby's neck, left shoulder, and left ankle throbbed.

At the moment, though, Colby was more worried about his friends. As Colby reached Tom, he discovered that the worst had happened. Tom's body was still. His face was covered with ice. He was dead.

DECIDING TO SURVIVE

Though he was hurt and heartbroken, Colby made an important decision. He set aside his pain and sadness and focused on finding a way off the mountain. He thought about his mother, who had raised her children alone. Colby was close to his mother.

Colby snapped this photo of himself on the mountain. He knew it might be the last one ever taken of him.

He didn't want to die on the mountain without having the chance to say good-bye.

Colby had no radio to call for help. He and his friends had decided not to take one. They believed climbers should survive on skill, not technology.

Colby's mittens and left crampon were lost in the fall. He took Tom's crampon and attached it to his left boot. He then took a bag of ice screws hanging around Tom's neck. He also picked up Tom's pack, which held his bivvy bag. Finally, he cut Tom's rope right above the point it connected to Colby's harness. Colby knew the rope would be handy as he climbed down the mountain. But when Colby cut the rope, Tom's body and his rope tumbled downward. Colby watched in horror as Tom fell out of sight.

Colby realized his weakness and injuries had caused him to make the mistake of cutting the rope. He needed to rest and get warm. Colby crawled into Tom's bivvy bag. He huddled inside it the rest of the night as the freezing wind whipped around him.

EDGE FACT

The 1992 climbing season was deadly in Alaska. Eleven people had died on nearby Mount McKinley before Colby and his friends began their trip.

Colby struggled to reach a flat area where he could set up a tent.

SEARCHING FOR A FRIEND

The next morning, the wind died down. Colby set off to look for Ritt. He used two axes to anchor a rope into the ice as he painfully worked his way downward. Colby found Ritt's body 140 feet (43 meters) below.

Feelings of despair exploded inside Colby. Ritt was his college roommate and best friend. Now he was dead.

Colby reminded himself to focus on staying alive. He tried to get Ritt's equipment pack but knocked the body loose, sending it 30 feet (9.1 meters) down. Colby dropped down to Ritt's body and got water, food, fuel, and the tent. He took a drink, then struggled back up to his bivvy bag and axes.

PAINFUL PROGRESS

Colby headed for a flat area where he could set up a small camp. The distance was only about the length of two football fields, but it took him nearly a day to get there. Once there, he set up the tent and stove.

Colby used ice tools like these to get down the mountain.

After a supper of soup and melted snow, Colby tried to lie down and sleep. But every time he leaned back, a sharp pain shot through his neck. He couldn't sleep at all. The pain was simply too much. But he needed to rest, so he stayed there until morning.

After a breakfast of instant oatmeal, Colby headed to the top of a ridge. From there, he could go down. Using the crampons on his boots and an ice tool in each hand, Colby moved just a few inches at a time. The slow process was exhausting. Usually, Colby's body worked automatically when climbing or descending a mountain. But now his injuries worked against him.

THE DANGER CONTINUES

By the next morning, Colby could see the base camp 6 miles (9.6 kilometers) away. He was on the third day of his escape down the mountain. But his ordeal wasn't over yet.

During the next two days, Colby had some close calls. He slipped on an icy slope and started falling. Below was a 1,000-foot (300-meter) drop-off. He desperately swung his ax into the ice, stopping his fall and saving his life.

The next day, Colby was nearly buried in a second avalanche. He had been traveling down a slope when the snow started cracking and shifting. Terrified, he headed back up the slope and found another route down.

OFF THE MOUNTAIN

On the evening of June 23, Colby reached the Kahiltna Glacier. At last, he was off the mountain. When he arrived at the spot where the climbers had left their equipment, Colby put on his skis. He also put some of his gear in the small plastic sled.

Colby's final stop, base camp, was 4 miles (6.4 kilometers) away. It would be a dangerous trip. Glaciers like Kahiltna contain many crevasses, or deep cracks. Adventurers usually travel across glaciers tied together. That way, if one person falls in, the others can pull him or her out. Traveling alone, Colby moved slowly and carefully. He used his ski pole to poke at the snow in front of him.

Deep, dangerous crevasses cut into Kahiltna Glacier.

"THEY'RE NOT COMING BACK"

When Colby finally reached base camp, it was early in the morning. Colby dragged his left foot. His left arm was curled like a claw. The few people who were out didn't notice anything unusual about him. Climbers often looked ragged after a long, hard trip.

By now it was June 24. Colby headed straight for Tom's tent. He dug up the pot of spaghetti and ate it cold, not bothering to heat up the stove. Colby rested for several hours before hobbling over to the shelter of Annie Duquette, the woman who ran the camp.

"What happened to you?" Annie asked. "Where are the other two?"

Colby began to cry. "They're not coming back."

"What happened to you? Where are the other two?"

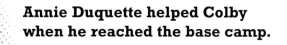
Annie Duquette helped Colby when he reached the base camp.

CHAPTER 4

OVERCOMING TRAGEDY

LEARN ABOUT:
- STUCK IN CAMP
- BACK TO CLIMBING
- LIFE TODAY

Annie kept Colby in her shelter. She radioed for help, but no planes could land. About 250 miles (400 kilometers) to the south, Mount Spurr had just erupted. The volcano spewed a cloud of ash 9 miles (14 kilometers) into the sky. All nearby airports were closed.

Annie took care of Colby for the next four days. On June 28, a plane took Colby to a hospital in Anchorage, Alaska. There, doctors treated Colby's broken neck, ankle, and shoulder blade.

Mount Spurr's eruption kept Colby at the base camp for several days.

27

Colby spent 10 days in the hospital. He then stayed at his mother's home in Massachusetts. After three months in a wheelchair, Colby was able to walk on his own. Less than one year after the accident, he was climbing again.

By 1993, Colby was climbing mountains again.

28

STILL CLIMBING

With his wife, Caitlin Palmer, Colby runs an outdoor climbing school in Talkeetna, Alaska. He has written two books about mountain climbing in Alaska. Though Colby rarely talks about his accident, he does sometimes use it to teach his students about climbing safety.

No one can be sure why Colby survived the avalanche, while Ritt and Tom didn't. But there are reasons Colby survived his climb down the mountain. His expert climbing skills were one reason. Another was his extreme mental toughness. Though he was heartbroken by his friends' deaths, Colby didn't give up. He thought only about staying alive.

In 2005, Caitlin and Colby had a baby daughter, Lisle.

29

GLOSSARY

avalanche (AV-uh-lanch)—a large mass of ice, snow, or earth that suddenly moves down the side of a mountain

crampon (KRAMP-on)—a metal frame with pointed metal teeth that attaches to a climber's boot; crampons give climbers secure footing on snow and ice.

crevasse (kri-VAHSS)—a deep crack in a glacier

glacier (GLAY-shur)—a large, slow-moving sheet of ice and snow

ridge (RIJ)—an area of rock or earth that spikes out from a mountain

summit (SUHM-it)—the highest point of a mountain

taut (TAWT)—something that is pulled tight and straight

READ MORE

Hall, Margaret. *Denali National Park.* Symbols of Freedom. Chicago: Heinemann, 2006.

O'Shei, Tim. *The World's Most Amazing Survival Stories.* The World's Top Tens. Mankato, Minn.: Capstone Press, 2007.

Sandler, Michael. *Mountains: Surviving on Mount Everest.* X-treme Places. New York: Bearport, 2006.

INTERNET SITES

FactHound offers a safe, fun way to find Internet sites related to this book. All of the sites on FactHound have been researched by our staff.

Here's how:

1. Visit *www.facthound.com*

2. Choose your grade level.

3. Type in this book ID **0736867783** for age-appropriate sites. You may also browse subjects by clicking on letters, or by clicking on pictures and words.

31

4. Click on the **Fetch It** button.

FactHound will fetch the best sites for you!

INDEX